D0601652

Understanding the Elements of the Periodic Table™

PHOSPHORUS

Michael A. Sommers

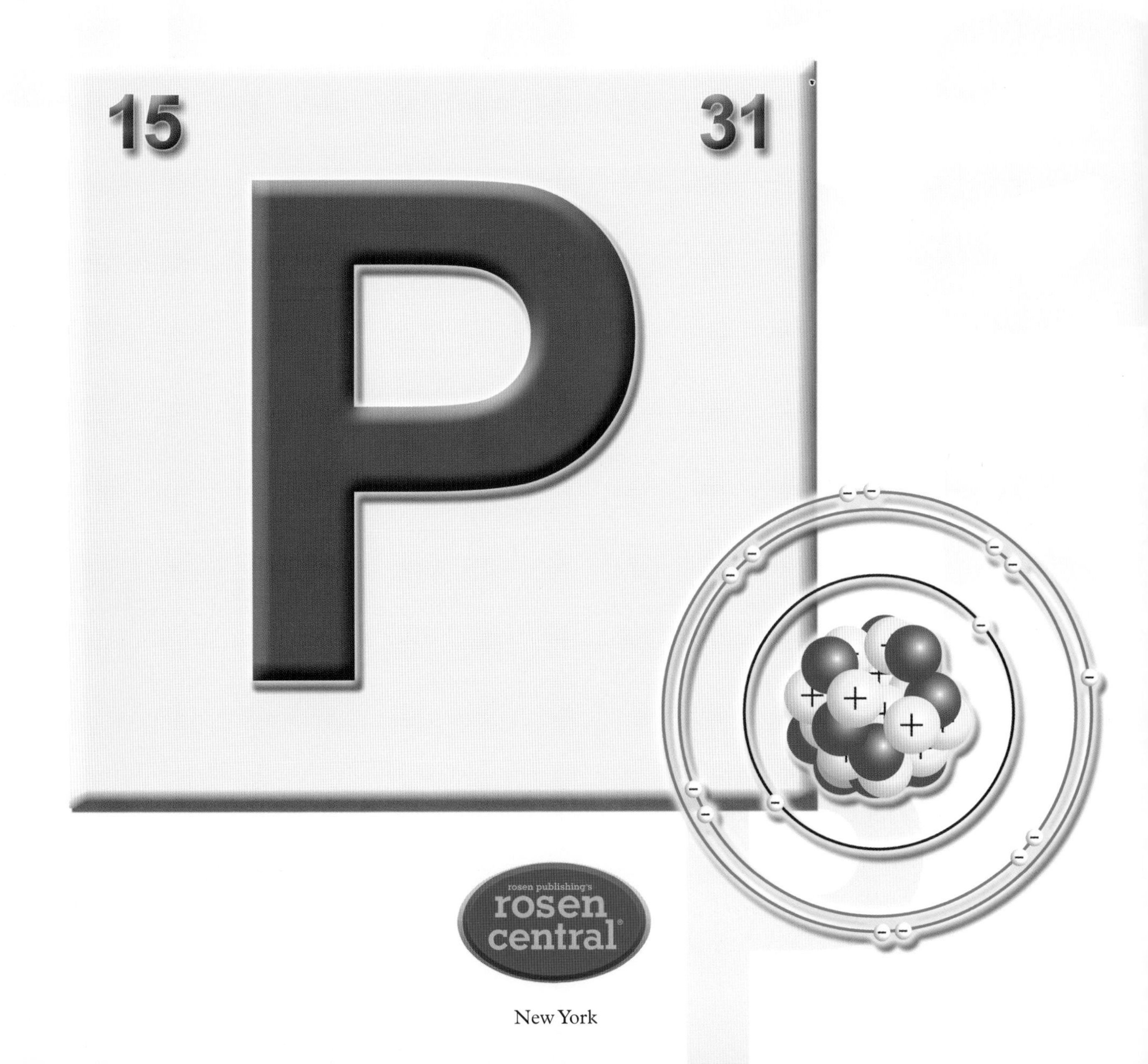

New York

Também pra Lui

Published in 2008 by The Rosen Publishing Group, Inc.
29 East 21st Street, New York, NY 10010

First Edition

Library of Congress Cataloging-in-Publication Data

Sommers, Michael A., 1966–
Phosphorus / Michael A. Sommers.
p. cm.—(Understanding the elements of the periodic table)
Includes bibliographical references and index.
ISBN-13: 978-1-4042-1960-1
ISBN-10: 1-4042-1960-9
1. Phosphorus. 2. Phosphorus compounds. I. Title.
QD181.P1S66 2008
546'.712—dc22

2007002815

Manufactured in China

On the cover: Phosphorus's square on the periodic table of elements. Inset: Model of phosphorus's subatomic structure.

Contents

Introduction

If you take a look around you right this minute, you can probably see hundreds of different things. You'll see your arms, this book, maybe some furniture, a room, friends, and possibly a window that looks out onto trees, grass, buildings, clouds, the sun (or moon, if you're a night reader), and the sky. What do all these things have in common? They consist of matter. Matter is anything that takes up space and has mass (or weight). As such, everything on Earth—and in the entire universe—is made up of matter. But what is matter made of?

Over 2,000 years ago, the ancient Greeks asked themselves this very same question. The answer they came up with was that all matter was made up of four elements: earth, air, water, and fire. Centuries later, chemists—chemistry being the study of matter and the changes that affect it—discovered that there were many more than four elements. In fact, to date, more than 100 elements have been identified.

Today we know that elements are all around us. They are the basic building blocks of matter and they exist as solids, liquids, and gases. You are probably familiar with many elements already. You see them, touch them, and even use them on a daily basis. Copper—present in pennies, nickels, dimes, and quarters—is an element. So is the silver that is in your earrings, belt buckles, and forks. And of course, if it weren't for the element oxygen, we wouldn't even be breathing.

This photograph shows the bright light and sparks, as well as the white smoke, given off by the chemical reaction that occurs when phosphorus comes into contact with oxygen.

One of the most important elements is phosphorus. Unlike elements such as gold, copper, or aluminum, chances are you haven't encountered phosphorus in its pure state. However, whether you know it or not, phosphorus is quite present in our lives. For instance, every time you strike a match, you are using phosphorus. This is because phosphorus, which burns very easily, is the main ingredient in match heads and on the sides of matchboxes.

Phosphorus has been lighting up people's lives for a long time. In fact, the name of the element itself comes from Greek and means "bearer of light" (in ancient Greek, *phos* meant "light" and *phorus* referred to a carrier or transporter). The Greeks referred to the planet Venus as "phosphorus" because it appeared as a bright light in the night sky. A few centuries later, the Romans adopted the word "phosphorus," which in Latin came to mean "morning star."

All these associations of phosphorus with bright, burning lights are not surprising. One of the most apparent defining characteristics of this element is the glow it gives off whenever it comes into contact with oxygen. For this reason, it was one of the first chemical elements to be discovered.

However, phosphorus is much more than just a glow-in-the-dark substance. It is an extremely useful element present in everything from matchbooks and fireworks to steel, bronze, fertilizers, pesticides, and even toothpaste. It is also an essential part of all living things. We humans, for example, have phosphorus in our bones, nerve tissue, and cells, and even in our DNA.

Chapter One
The History of Phosphorus

Phosphorus was the first of all the chemical elements whose discovery was recorded and whose discoverer was known. Scientific discoveries usually involve many strange and unlikely events. However, one of the strangest and most unlikely—not to mention a little disgusting—involves the discovery of phosphorus.

A Surprising Discovery

Hennig Brand (c. 1630–1710) was a German merchant and amateur alchemist. Like many European alchemists during this time period, he spent a lot of time—and most of his first wife's money—carrying out chemical experiments in the hopes of finding the legendary "philosopher's stone." (This stone was believed to be the secret for turning metals into gold.) By all accounts, he wasn't very successful as a merchant and the possibility of turning common substances into gold really motivated him.

In the 1660s, Brand became interested in combining his own urine with many other substances after reading a chemistry book that included a recipe for turning concentrated urine, alum (a type of aluminum), and potassium nitrate into silver. Of course, this recipe didn't work. However, Brand didn't give up. It also helped that after his first wife died, he married

This 1771 painting, *The Alchymist*, by English artist Joseph Wright, depicts an alchemist, perhaps Hennig Brand, discovering phosphorus in his search for the mythical philosopher's stone.

Alchemy

Before the development of modern chemistry, people who investigated chemical substances were known as alchemists. Beginning in ancient Egypt and the Middle East, alchemists carried out many experiments on basic elements in order to uncover mysteries of the universe and better understand different forms of matter. One of the alchemists' greatest preoccupations was finding a way of transforming common metals into silver or gold. During the Middle Ages in Europe, alchemists were particularly obsessed with finding a legendary substance known as the philosopher's stone.

again—this time to a wealthy widow whose finances allowed Brand to continue his investigations.

In 1669, Brand tried a new variation on his experiments. He collected sixty buckets of his urine and let them sit around for two weeks (he must have been a brave soul to have withstood the smell!). Then he gathered the concentrated urine samples together and boiled the liquid for twenty-four hours until it became a thick syrup. During the process, Brand was surprised to observe a glowing vaporous gas that rose up from the boiling urine. After this gas cooled and was collected in an airtight container, it formed a solid that continued to shine in the dark, giving off enough light for Brand to read one of his alchemy books. Stranger still was that this shiny snow-white substance burst into flames when it came into contact with the air.

Brand didn't know what he had made, but he was very excited. For a while, he thought the glow-in-the-dark, explosive substance was magical. In reality, however, he had discovered phosphorus!

The Secret Spreads

Most alchemists kept the details of their experiments secret, and Hennig Brand was no exception. For a time, he continued to experiment with phosphorus, still hoping that it would somehow turn into gold. When all his efforts proved to be in vain, he decided to try to make some money from his discovery in another way. In 1675, he sold his secret recipe to a German physician named Johannes Daniel Kraft, who subsequently showed off the wondrous substance around the courts of Europe. Before long, the secret that it was made from urine leaked out and other scientists began trying to make their own phosphorus.

Among the first to succeed was the Irish scientist Robert Boyle (1627–1691), who is now generally regarded as the first modern chemist. However, it was Boyle's assistant, Ambrose Godfrey, who (after visiting Brand in 1679) developed a method for making phosphorus on a large scale. Godfrey became the first manufacturer of phosphorus, which he sold throughout England and the rest of Europe. Unfortunately, he wasn't always careful in handling the highly flammable element. Godfrey's fingers were constantly burned and blistered and his clothes frequently sported burn holes. However, his method of producing phosphorus by evaporating urine was in general use until the late 1700s. And despite the damage to his hands and clothing, manufacturing phosphorus also made him a tidy profit.

One of the First Elements

Around the same time that Brand was discovering phosphorus in Germany, other important discoveries concerning chemical elements were taking place in the neighboring country of France. The author of these discoveries—and the notion of what a chemical element was and wasn't—was a French nobleman and scientist named Antoine-Laurent de Lavoisier (1743–1794).

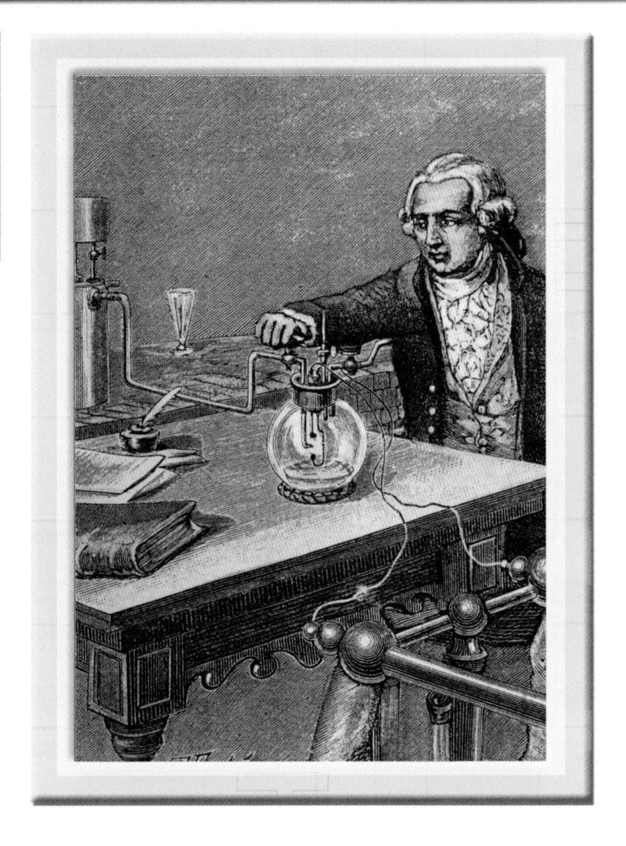

Antoine-Laurent de Lavoisier was one of the great scientific minds of the eighteenth century. Some of his most important chemical experiments dealt with the reactions of burning elements.

Considered the father of modern chemistry, Lavoisier discovered and named the elements hydrogen (H) and oxygen (O). He also invented a list of thirty-three elements that was a model for the periodic table. Among these elements—which included sulfur (S), zinc (Zn), and mercury (Hg)—was the newly discovered phosphorus (P).

It was Lavoisier who invented the definition of an element as any substance that could not be broken down into a simpler unit. For example, he discovered that water (H_2O) wasn't an element since it could be broken down into two other substances: hydrogen and oxygen. In order to determine whether a substance was an element or not, Lavoisier carried out many tests. These included heating and cooling, filtering, and reacting substances with other substances such as acids. Substances that could not be broken down or transformed were considered to be elements. This was the case with phosphorus.

The Periodic Table

In 1869, a Russian chemistry professor named Dmitry Mendeleyev (1834–1907) was one of the first people to organize the chemical elements into a chart. Known as the periodic table of elements, this simple one-page chart arranged all the elements according to their atomic weight, from lightest to heaviest. It also offered a lot of basic information so his students would be able to identify and understand the elements' behaviors. Over the past 150 years, new information has emerged, along with the discovery of many more elements. The basic layout of Mendeleyev's original table, however, continues to be used by scientists and students around the world.

Reading a Periodic Table

The periodic table is a very useful guide to the elements. When you first take a look at one, your eye will most likely focus on the large one-, two-, and three-letter symbols that represent each element. Most of these are abbreviations of the element's English name—such as S for sulfur and O for oxygen. Phosphorus, with the symbol P, is easy to identify. Others are more difficult because their abbreviations come from other languages, particularly Latin. Ag, for example, stands for *argentum*, which is the Latin word for silver. Meanwhile, the symbol for potassium is K, which comes from *kalium*. Other elements are named after the place they were discovered or the person who discovered them. Europium (Eu), for example, is named after the European continent. Rutherfordium (Rf) is named after Lord Rutherford, a famous chemist from New Zealand.

The symbol for the element phosphorus is P. The number on the left is its atomic number: 15. The number on the right, 31, refers to its atomic weight, or mass.

Reading the periodic table is quite straightforward. Each box shows an element's symbol, along with its atomic weight and number. The atomic number allows you to

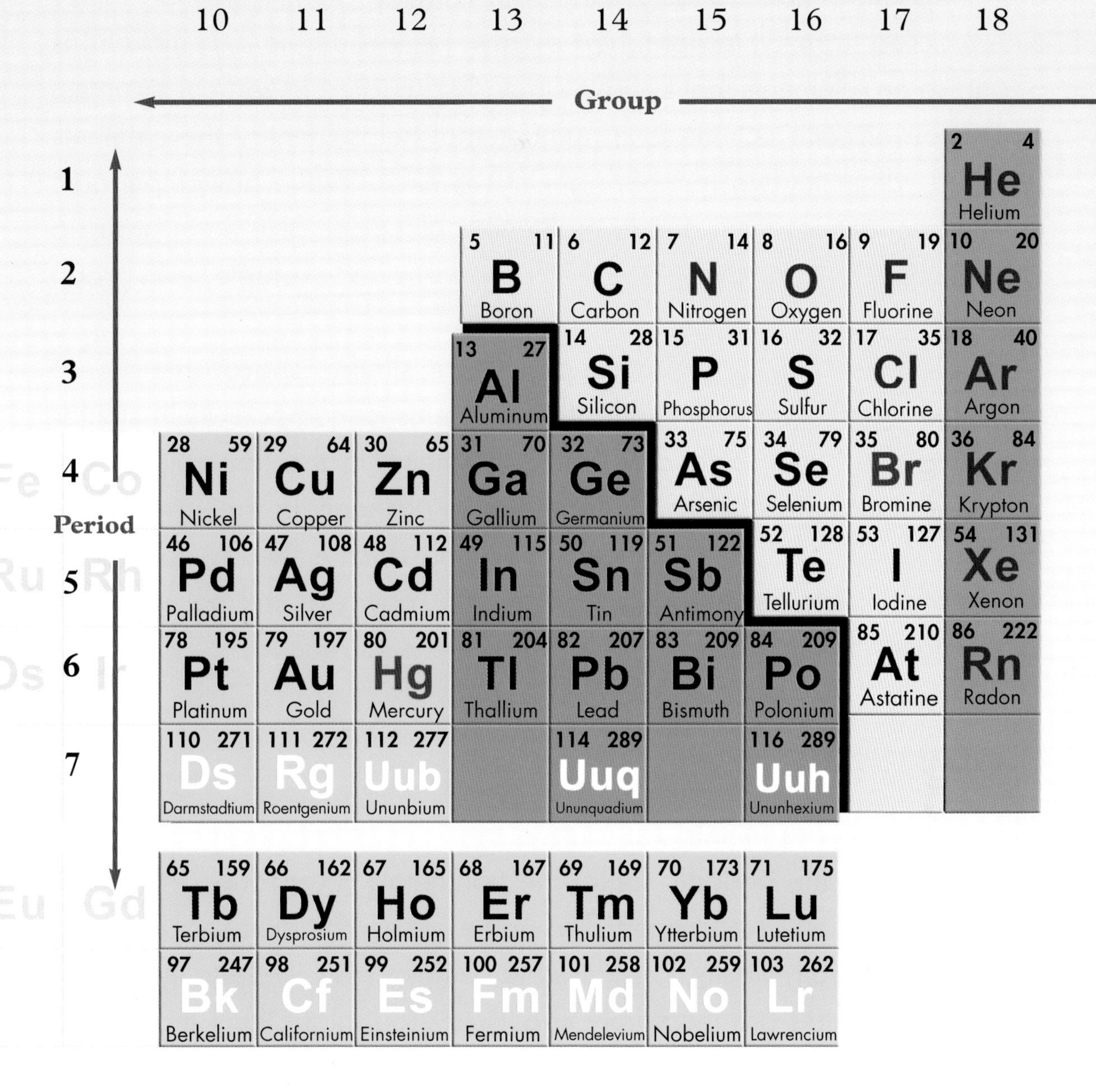

Groups 10 (VIIIB) through 18 (O) of the periodic table are displayed above. Visible in bold black is the zigzagging "staircase" that separates metallic elements from semimetals and nonmetals.

identify the element and also determines its location. Atomic numbers begin at the top left of the table beginning with H (hydrogen), which is 1. They then proceed from left to right, row by row. He (helium) is 2, Li (lithium) is 3, and so on. Elements that behave similarly are listed in vertical columns. At the top of each column is a number that helps identify the elements grouped within it. Two numbering systems exist. While newer periodic tables label groups from one to eighteen, older ones give each group a Roman numeral followed by a letter. Phosphorus, for example, is in group 15 or VA.

The elements in a group usually share similar characteristics, or properties. They often react with other elements or compounds in similar ways. Each group has its own name. Elements in the first column are known as alkali metals, for example, while elements in the seventeenth column are halogens. The eighteenth column, which is the last column on the periodic table, is made up of elements known as the noble gases. What makes them unique is that they are the least reactive.

Nonmetals

Many elements are metals, but only a few—including phosphorus—are nonmetals. On the periodic table, the nonmetals are grouped together, with the exception of hydrogen. The noble gases (the elements in group 18 or O) are also typically considered to be nonmetals. Despite their small number, nonmetals are incredibly important. You might think that metals such as silver and gold are precious, but it is nonmetals such as phosphorus, oxygen, carbon, and nitrogen that make up the fundamental matter that creates life on Earth.

Chapter Two
The Atom Explained

In the last chapter, you learned that elements are the building blocks of matter. But what are elements themselves made of? In the eighteenth century, scientists began to suspect that elements were made of tiny particles they called atoms. The word "atom" comes from the Greek term *atamos*, meaning "uncuttable." It refers to the fact that atoms are the basic units that make up elements and can't be divided (or cut) into smaller parts that still retain the fundamental properties of that element.

The Atom

John Dalton (1766–1844), an English chemist, came up with the idea of atoms in order to explain why elements always reacted the way they did. Dalton believed that all elements were made up of unique types of atoms. Atoms from one element could join together with atoms from another element to form more complex compounds.

Once it had been discovered that elements were made up of atoms, chemists began to investigate what atoms themselves were made of. By the early twentieth century, they had determined the answer: every atom consists of three basic particles—protons, neutrons, and electrons. In fact, it is the number of electrons, protons, and neutrons in each element that distinguishes it from another.

ELEMENTS

	W.t		W.t
Hydrogen.	1	Strontian	46
Azote	5	Barytes	68
Carbon	54	Iron	50
Oxygen	7	Zinc	56
Phosphorus	9	Copper	56
Sulphur	13	Lead	90
Magnesia	20	Silver	190
Lime	24	Gold	190
Soda	28	Platina	190
Potash	42	Mercury	167

This diagram is the table of elements developed by English chemist John Dalton in 1808. The table was the first to make reference to the existence of atoms as essential building blocks of each element.

Protons

Protons are particles with a positive charge (shown by the symbol "+"). Along with neutrons, they make up the center of the atom. The central core of an atom is called the nucleus. It is the number of protons in an atom (the atomic number) that defines an individual element. This number of protons also explains an element's location on the periodic table. If you look at a periodic table you will notice that an atom of phosphorus, the fifteenth element, always has fifteen protons. If you could take away one proton, you wouldn't have phosphorus anymore, but silicon (Si), which has fourteen protons. Adding one proton would give you the element sulfur (S), which has sixteen protons.

Neutrons

Like their name suggests, neutrons are particles with a neutral charge. Instead of having a positive or negative charge, they have a charge of zero. Neutrons bind protons together. Without them, protons would not stay together because particles with the same charge (whether positive or negative) push each other away.

If you've ever held the same poles of two magnets together, you will have observed how particles with the same charge repel each other. Repelling, or pushing away, is the opposite of attraction. Attraction occurs when particles (or magnets) with two opposite charges ("+" and "–") are brought together. Neutrons are essential because they neutralize, or cancel out, protons' tendency to repel each other. The presence of neutrons therefore allows the particles in the nucleus to stay close together.

Electrons

Electrons are negatively charged particles (represented by the "–" sign) that are much smaller and lighter than protons and neutrons. They are attracted to the positively charged protons in the nucleus and orbit the

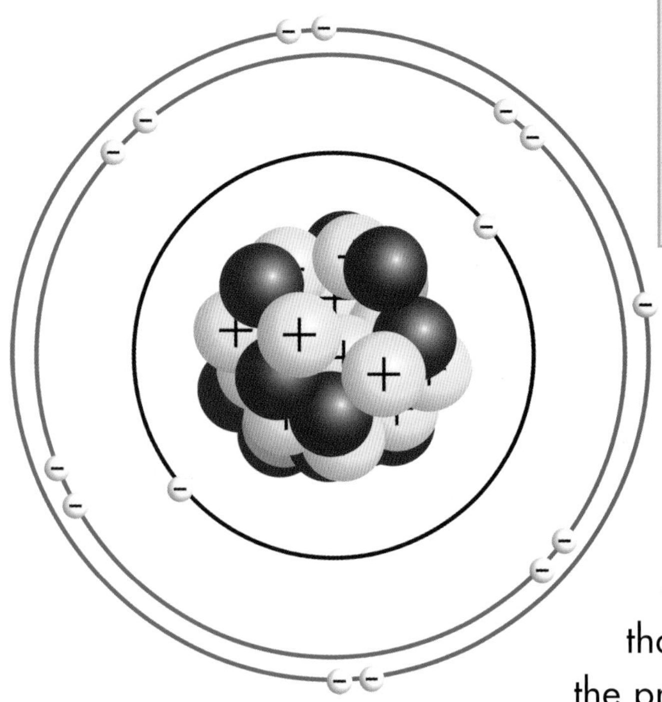

This is a diagram of a phosphorus atom. Positively charged protons cluster in the nucleus, along with neutral neutrons. Tiny negatively charged electrons spin around the nucleus in shells.

atom's nucleus at very high speeds. In fact, in one second, an electron can spin around a nucleus one billion times. Together, the electrons in an atom create a negative charge that balances the positive charge of the protons in the atom's nucleus.

Electrons spin around the nucleus in overlapping regions. Atoms can have between one and seven shells of electrons. Electrons located in inner shells are strongly attracted to the nucleus by the protons. The attractive forces that bind electrons in outer shells to the nucleus are much weaker. The higher the atomic number of an element, the more shells and electrons it will have.

An atom of phosphorus has fifteen protons, sixteen neutrons, and fifteen electrons. The electrons are in three shells: the first shell has two electrons; the second has eight; the third has five.

Chemical Bonding

The electrons in an atom's outermost shell are known as valence electrons. They have a special role because they allow chemical bonding between elements. Chemical bonding is the joining together of two or more atoms. For instance, water (H_2O) is the result of the bonding together of two hydrogen (H) atoms with an oxygen (O) atom. In nature, phosphorus is

Phosphorus P Snapshot

15 P 31

Chemical Symbol:	P
Classification:	Nonmetal
Properties:	White phosphorus: Soft, white, waxy solid; extremely flammable (bursts into flames on contact with air); strong garlicky odor Red phosphorus: brownish red powder, quite stable, doesn't dissolve in most solvents Black phosphorus: black solid, very stable, doesn't dissolve in most solvents
Discovered by:	Hennig Brand
Atomic Number:	15
Average Atomic Weight:	30.97376 amu
Protons:	15
Electrons:	15
Neutrons:	16
Phase at Room Temperature:	Solid
Density at 68° Fahrenheit (20° Celsius):	1.82 g/cm^3 (white phosphorus); 2.34 g/cm^3 (red phosphorus); 2.69 g/cm^3 (black phosphorus)
Melting Point:	111.7°F (44.3°C; 317.3 K)
Boiling Point:	536°F (280°C; 553 K)
Commonly Found:	In phosphate rock (United States, Russia, North Africa)

always in compounds, mixed with other elements. Elements with which phosphorus combines most frequently are oxygen and hydrogen.

The first eighteen elements on the periodic table can hold up to eight electrons in their valence shells. Phosphorus's outermost shell has five electrons. This means that it is unstable. An atom is unstable when there is not enough binding energy to hold the nucleus together. To become stable, phosphorus atoms require three more electrons. The way an atom does this is by sharing electrons with atoms from other elements, which is an example of bonding. Phosphorus can create bonds with three different atoms at the same time. The result is that phosphorus can form a wide variety of stable compounds.

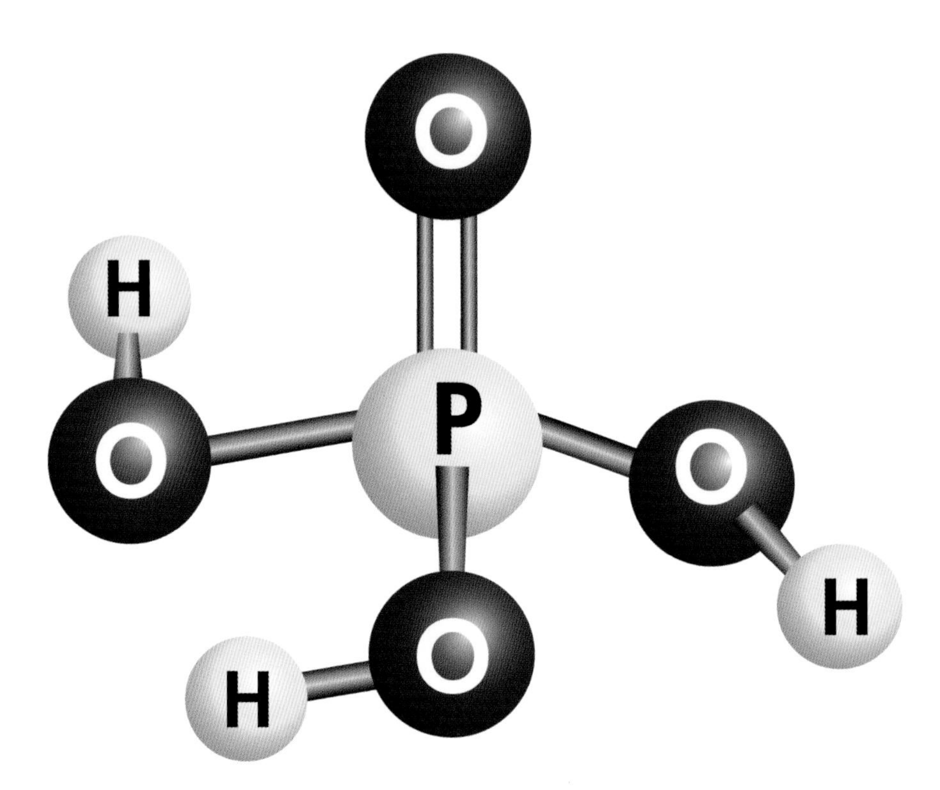

This diagram shows an example of chemical bonding. Four oxygen (O) atoms and three hydrogen (H) atoms bond with one atom of phosphorus (P) to form the compound phosphoric acid (H_3PO_4).

Atomic Weight and Number

Each box on the periodic table has two numbers. The smaller number is the atomic number, which shows the number of protons in an atom of that element. For example, since one atom of phosphorus contains fifteen protons, the atomic number of phosphorus is 15. The second, larger number on the table shows an element's average atomic weight, measured in atomic mass units (amu). This weight is calculated by adding together the number of protons and neutrons in one atom. The weight is average, and not exact, because an element's atoms are not always completely identical. Many times, they consist of isotopes. An isotope is an atom with the same number of protons as the atomic number, but a different number of neutrons. Phosphorus, for example, has only one isotope. In fact, all phosphorus atoms have sixteen neutrons, instead of fifteen—making a total of thirty-one nuclear particles (fifteen protons and sixteen neutrons). Consequently, the atomic weight of phosphorus is 30.97 amu. This is rounded up to 31 amu.

Chapter Three
Properties of Phosphorus

It is rare to go walking through the countryside and stumble across an element in its pure form. Even elements such as silver and gold are often found as tiny particles of rocks, mixed together with many other elements. So how do you go about recognizing an element?

Scientists identify an element by examining the properties that distinguish it from all other elements. Properties refer to the characteristics or traits of an element. For instance, gold and pyrite (known as fool's gold) resemble each other because they both share the property of having a brassy yellow color. However, in terms of many other properties they are quite different. Fool's gold, for example, is much harder, less dense, and more brittle than real gold. If you rub it against a piece of paper, it will leave a greenish-black streak, whereas real gold will leave a golden-yellow streak. As you can see, knowing an element's properties and how to identify them is really important—after all, who would want to mistake fool's gold for real gold?

Some properties can be measured using scientific tools and equipment. Others can be observed merely by looking at the element, or by carrying out experiments and watching the changes and reactions that occur. By measuring and observing the properties of any sample of matter—whether a solid, liquid, or gas—you can tell what kinds of element it contains.

Observing and Measuring Phosphorus

Phosphorus is an unusual element because as a solid, it exists in three forms: white, red, and black.

White Phosphorus

The most common form of phosphorus is white phosphorus, which, at room temperature is a soft, waxy solid. As Hennig Brand discovered, white phosphorus glows in the dark and has a strong, unpleasant smell that is often described as resembling garlic. The other highly observable property of white phosphorus is its flammability. A flammable substance is one that can very easily explode into flames. White phosphorus self-ignites whenever it comes into contact with air, making it extremely dangerous to handle. For this reason, whenever white phosphorus is stored or transported, it is usually placed in water to isolate it from the air.

If you were to run experiments on white phosphorus, you would discover some more interesting properties about this unique element. For instance, you wouldn't have to turn up the heat too high in order to get phosphorus to melt from a solid into a liquid. This is because phosphorus melts at a temperature of 111.7 degrees Fahrenheit (44.3 degrees Celsius). A significantly higher temperature, however, is needed to change phosphorus from a solid to a gas. The boiling point for phosphorus is 536.0°F (280.0°C).

Red and Black Phosphorus

White phosphorus, heated in the absence of air, results in the conversion to red phosphorus. Less common than white phosphorus, at room temperature this form of phosphorus is a reddish brown powder. Despite the more vibrant color, red phosphorus behaves more calmly than its white cousin. Red phosphorus doesn't glow in the dark and it only catches fire when

The test tube on the left shows a sample of white phosphorus (safely stored in water so that it won't ignite). On the right is a (less dangerous) sample of red phosphorus.

exposed to the air at temperatures above 464°F (240°C), a fairly rare occurrence on this planet. As such, red phosphorus is more stable—and less dangerous—than white phosphorus, which self-ignites in the air at only 104°F (40°C).

Black phosphorus is the least reactive—and thus the least dangerous—of all the forms of phosphorus. For this reason, it is fairly uncommon since it has no commercial use. Black phosphorus is also made by heating white phosphorus at high temperatures, under lots of pressure. In its most common form, it appears as a black solid and resembles graphite (the material used in pencils).

Let It Glow

Phosphorus's glow-in-the-dark properties have attracted a lot of attention ever since the element was discovered in the seventeenth century. In fact, back then, phosphorus was a novelty item that went on tour around Europe so that kings and queens and their curious subjects could marvel at the strange greenish light it gave off. From early times, scientists knew that if the phosphorus was isolated in a sealed container such as a jar, its glow would last quite a while. However, for another 300 years, scientists couldn't completely explain what made the glow occur.

Finally, in 1974, two chemists named R. J. Van Zee and A. U. Khan discovered the secret of the glow: it was the result of phosphorus consuming oxygen. This "consumption" occurred when phosphorus—in solid or liquid form—came into contact with oxygen. Because this reaction was slow, in a sealed jar, the glow could continue for some time. The glow from this reaction is known as chemoluminescence. Chemoluminescence shouldn't be confused with phosphorescence, a term derived from phosphorus. Phosphorescence describes a substance—such as glow-in-the-dark stickers or the hands on a clock—that shines in the dark by re-emitting light that it has absorbed.

How Phosphorus Reacts

Phosphorus—particularly white phosphorus—is an extremely reactive element. This means that it forms chemical bonds very easily with many other elements. In fact, on Earth, phosphorus is never found alone in nature, but is always combined with other elements. Phosphorus reacts with elements such

This 1942 photograph was taken inside a phosphorus factory in Muscle Shoals, Alabama. The worker is melting down phosphate rocks in a large electric furnace in order to make pure phosphorus.

as chlorine (Cl), hydrogen (H), sulfur (S), sodium (Na), and calcium (Ca) to make many useful industrial products. However, the most common—and also the most potentially dangerous—element with which phosphorus reacts is oxygen. The air contains 21 percent oxygen. And when white phosphorus comes into contact with air containing oxygen, it can spontaneously ignite, meaning it explodes into flames.

Where Does Phosphorus Come From?

Phosphorus is found only in compounds with other elements. As a result, you can encounter it in many different types of minerals. One of the major

One of the most common forms of phosphate rock is apatite, shown here. Aside from its presence in many types of rocks, apatite is the mineral that makes up the teeth and bones of all vertebrate animals.

sources of phosphorus is phosphate rocks. Phosphate is a very common compound that combines phosphorus and oxygen atoms together in solid form. One of the biggest sources of phosphorus is apatite, a phosphate rock that also contains the element calcium. Large deposits of apatite can be found in China, Russia, and Morocco as well as the states of Florida, Tennessee, Utah, and Idaho.

Aside from rocks, much of the earth's soil and the bottom of the ocean contain phosphates. Phosphates provide soil with essential nutrients, which help plants to grow and develop. In the ocean, all marine creatures also depend upon phosphates. In turn, mammals that eat plants, fish, and seafood end up ingesting these life-giving phosphates.

Phosphorus and You

Phosphorus is essential for all living creatures, including human beings. In fact, we can't live without it. Phosphorus is in many of the compounds—particularly phosphates—that help us to store energy in our bodies. Every time you eat something, you are taking in energy from these phosphorus compounds that helps your internal organs to keep working. Phosphorus is an important ingredient in our cells, genes (our DNA), nerve tissue, blood,

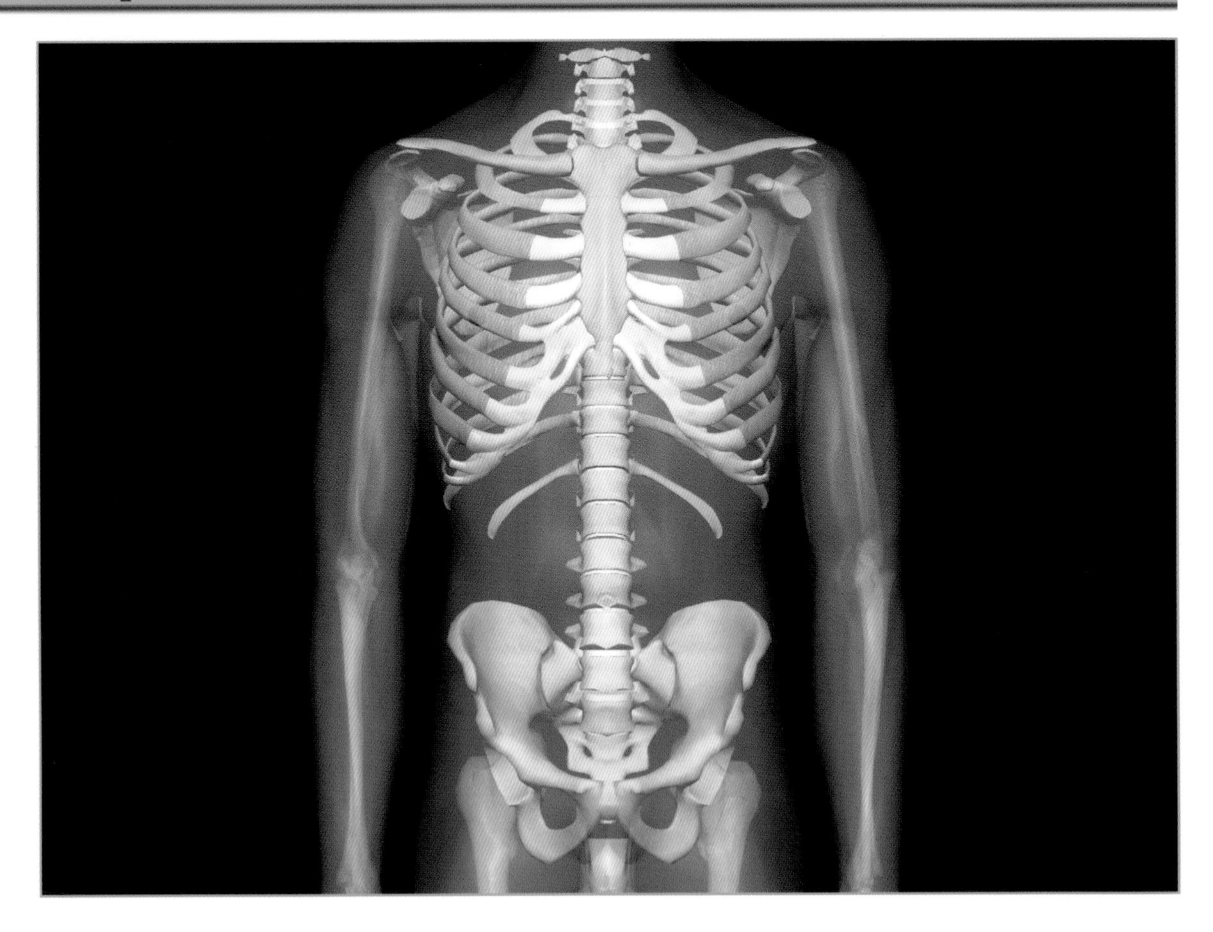

Phosphorus is an important part of the human body's bones. Phosphate additives in food make up 10 percent of the phosphates consumed by the average American. The other 90 percent comes naturally from meats and vegetables.

and bones. In fact, about 85 percent of the phosphorus present in our bodies is combined with the calcium that forms our teeth and bones.

We obtain the phosphates our bodies need naturally, from eating foods (plants and animals) that contain phosphorus. Every day, an adult in the industrialized world, who has a balanced diet, eats and eliminates between 0.03 and 0.1 ounces (1 to 3 grams) of phosphates. However, if you don't ingest enough of this essential element, don't worry: your body will pick up the slack by naturally creating reserves of phosphates in the blood and bones. Ultimately, on any given day, an average person has about 2 pounds (0.9 kg) of phosphorus in his or her body.

Chapter Four
Phosphorus Compounds

Phosphorus is found throughout the universe. It is present in the sun's atmosphere and in the meteorites that hurtle through space. Here on our planet, phosphorus makes up around 0.1 percent of Earth's crust.

Phosphates

As you saw in the previous chapter, one of the most basic and important phosphorus compounds is phosphate (PO_4^{3-}). It is a mixture of phosphorus and oxygen that is present in soil, rocks, and ocean beds, and it is one of the essential components of all living things. It is also a useful form of phosphorus for a variety of industries and products.

Currently, millions of tons of phosphate rocks are mined throughout the world every year. Some of the largest phosphate mines in the world are in North Africa. There are even enormous phosphate mines in the Sahara Desert. After they are mined, over 90 percent of all phosphate rocks are ground down into particles. They are further processed or combined with other substances to be made into a variety of products. Only around 10 percent of phosphate is purified into elemental phosphorus. To get pure phosphorus, phosphate rocks are heated to melting point in a gigantic electric furnace. Unwanted material falls to the bottom of the furnace,

This aerial photograph shows phosphate mines located in the Sahara Desert. One of the most arid and uninhabitable regions on the planet, the Sahara is also one of the world's richest phosphate sources.

while elemental phosphorus becomes a gas that can be further separated and collected as white phosphorus.

Fertilizers

One of the biggest uses of phosphates is in fertilizers. By the late 1700s, scientists had discovered that plants depended on phosphorus in the soil in order to grow well. Across Europe, farmers began to use crushed animal bones and guano (the phosphorus-rich excrement of birds and bats) to help their crops grow. This knowledge, in turn, led to the development of the fertilizer industry in the early 1800s. Phosphates from animal bones

Them Bones

When phosphorus first began to be made commercially in the nineteenth century, its source was no longer urine, but bones. In the eighteenth century, scientists had discovered that mammals' bones were high in calcium phosphates. Subsequently, bones were ground up and then treated with strong acids to obtain phosphates. If the phosphates were further heated until they gave off phosphorus vapors, pure white phosphorus—which was used by the match industry beginning in the 1830s—could be obtained. Although since the 1890s, the electric furnace has been used to process phosphate rocks (melting them down so impurities can be removed), bone ash is still used in the production of the finest china because of its strength and special shine.

and, later, phosphate rocks, were processed on a large scale and made into fertilizers. Since the second half of the twentieth century, global demand for fertilizers has led to enormous increases in phosphate production. These fertilizers can be made in solid and liquid form.

Phosphate fertilizers have advantages and disadvantages. On the positive side, fertilizers have increased agricultural production, which has helped to reduce hunger all over the world. However, phosphate rock mining methods have often led to the destruction of fragile ecosystems, causing damage to soil and plant life in various parts of the world. The way the phosphate is processed has also created environmental damage. After being mined, phosphate rocks need to be washed in order to remove unwanted substances such as clay. Unfortunately, these substances are often deposited in huge "slime ponds" that, if they flood, can end up polluting rivers and lakes and negatively affecting aquatic life.

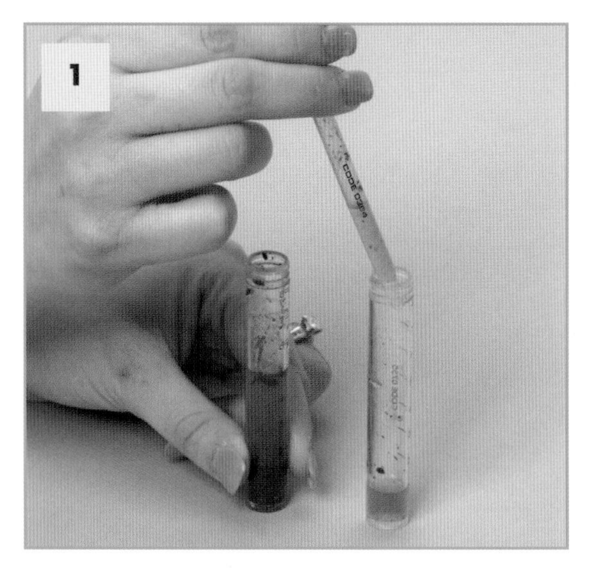

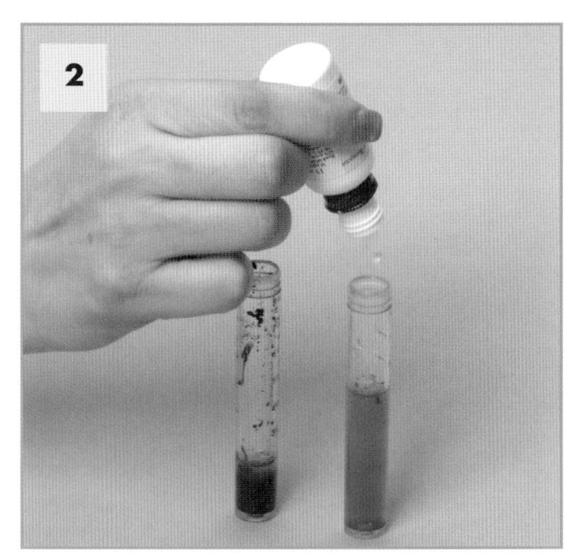

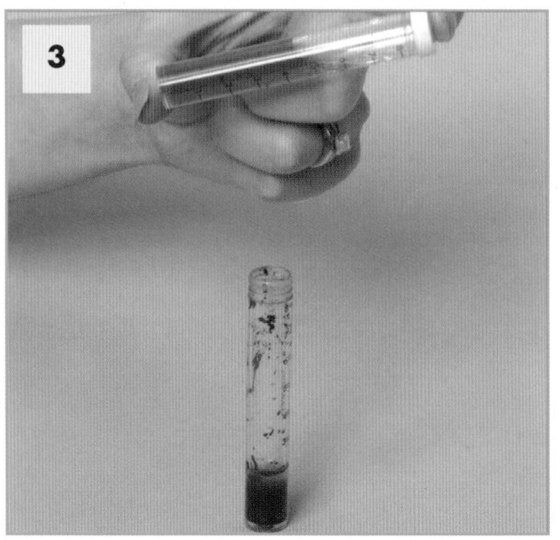

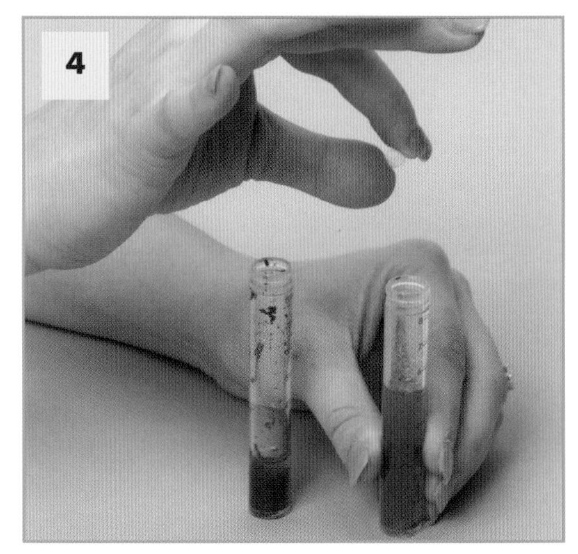

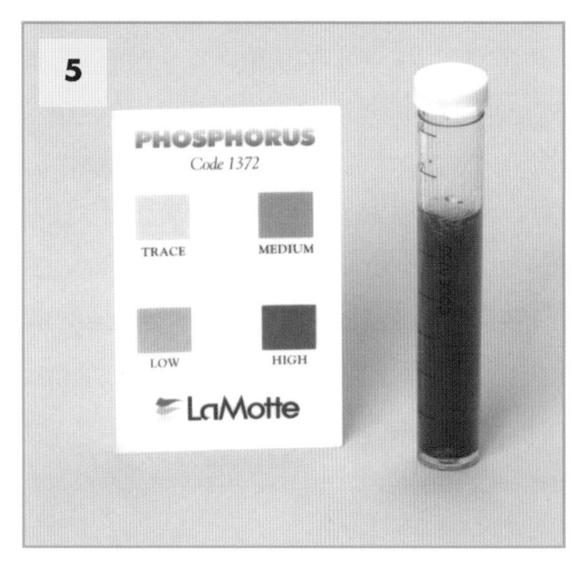

Phosphorus is a necessary element for healthy plant growth. A standard soil kit can be used to test for its presence in soil. Soil is mixed with a phosphorus extracting solution and allowed to settle. Then, the liquid above the soil is transferred to a clean test tube (1). Phosphorus indicator solution is added (2) and mixed (3). A phosphorus test tablet (4) is added to the mixture and shaken until the tablet dissolves. The end result is matched against the kit's phosphorus color chart (5).

Phosphoric Acid

Another important phosphorus compound is phosphoric acid (H_3PO_4). Phosphoric acid is also a compound of phosphorus with oxygen. Pure phosphoric acid is a colorless solid that resembles a crystal. For industrial use, it is melted in water into a syrupy solution.

The biggest use of phosphoric acid is in the fertilizer industry. However, it has many other uses as well. Because phosphorus is quite poisonous, phosphoric acid is used to make pesticides and insecticides that protect crops and kill unwanted critters. In the metal industry, it is used to remove rust and to polish metals such as aluminum (Al). Phosphoric acid is also an ingredient in some cleaning products.

Perhaps the use of phosphoric acid you are most familiar with is its addition to fizzy cola drinks. Believe it or not, it is diluted phosphoric acid that gives Coke, Pepsi, and other bubbly cola beverages their distinctive tangy taste.

You can tell if your soft drink contains phosphoric acid by doing a simple test. Choose an old, dull penny and drop it into a glass of cola. As you may know, pennies lose their shine over time because the copper (Cu) in them combines with oxygen in the air, turning their surfaces a dull brown. If you leave your penny in the glass overnight, when you fish it out the next morning, you will find that the previously dirty penny is bright and shiny! Chalk up this sudden cleanliness to phosphoric acid, which spent the night breaking up the oxygen-copper compound.

Phosphorus Salts

When phosphoric acids react with salt-based compounds containing sodium (Na), they create complex compounds known as phosphoric salts. These salts, which can dissolve in water, have many uses. They are used in the baking soda that helps breads and cakes to rise, as well as in

Like many laundry detergents, some of Tide's liquid detergents include complex sodium phosphates, which soften the laundry water during washing.

processed meats and cheeses. They are also used as supplements in animal feed. Even toothpaste contains phosphoric salts, since phosphorus helps makes bones and teeth strong.

One of the most common uses of phosphoric salts is in laundry soaps and detergents. These salts prevent scum from forming in the water and also stop dirt particles from sticking together. However, in some countries, including Switzerland, such salts have been banned from detergents since a number of scientists believe that the substances may harm the environment. The problem was that the phosphorus in the laundry water, after going down the drain, ended up in many lakes and rivers. People noticed that some lakes and rivers were turning green due to tiny plants called algae, which were growing out of control. The problem with the great numbers of algae was that they used up all the oxygen in the water, leaving fish to suffocate. The scientists put the blame for this situation on excess phosphorus. In the 1990s, it was discovered that other pollutants, and not phosphorus, were to blame for these occurrences. Nonetheless, although they're great at getting clothes clean, in many countries, phosphorus salts have been removed from detergents.

Chapter Five
Phosphorus in Our Lives

In the previous chapter, we took a look at some of the most common phosphorus compounds, along with how useful they have become to us. However, despite—and because—of its flammability, pure phosphorus also plays an important role in our lives. Although it is very dangerous, it also quite literally sets sparks flying!

White Phosphorus

Melting down phosphate rocks in an electric furnace and then separating out unwanted substances creates pure phosphorus. With further refining, one obtains white phosphorus. Because of its high flammability, white phosphorus is ideal for military uses. And since the early twentieth century, it has been used many times in war. White phosphorus is an important ingredient in fire bombs, smoke screens, explosives, and tracer bullets (bullets that give off sparks like fireworks, which come in handy if someone is ever lost in the wilderness and hoping to get rescued).

During World War I, white phosphorus was a key ingredient in a special fire bullet that was invented so that British soldiers could shoot down German zeppelins (balloon-like blimps) that flew over England. Like balloons, the German blimps were filled with hydrogen so they could float.

White phosphorus shells explode as American soldiers race across a street in Brest, France, during World War II. They are attempting to drive Nazi snipers from their hideouts.

Since hydrogen is extremely flammable when ignited, the phosphorus bullets were very effective. Two decades later, during World War II (1939–1945), phosphorus once again came to the aid of Allied troops. In England, phosphorus firebombs were given to specially chosen citizens for defense against German invaders.

Once phosphorus is ignited it is extremely hard to extinguish. As such, if and when it splashes onto skin, the effects are horrifying. In fact, during the world wars, people who suffered the effects of phosphorus bombs sometimes killed themselves rather than experience the terrible burning.

Poisonous Stuff

In addition to being highly flammable, white phosphorus is also very poisonous. In the early to mid-1800s when white phosphorus was used to make matches, there were tales of many accidental poisonings that occurred as a result of people breathing in the lethal fumes. Apparently, the white phosphorus in a single box of matches was enough to kill a person.

White phosphorus was an effective way of committing suicide as well as carrying out a murder, although it didn't always go undetected. There is a tale of a nineteenth-century woman who tried to murder her husband by putting white phosphorus in his food. Fortunately, at the last minute the victim was saved when he saw that his stew gave off a steam that glowed!

Matches

Before the nineteenth century, there was no easy or inexpensive way for people to light a fire when they wanted to do so. Rubbing two sticks or stones together wasn't exactly a

The matches pictured here were invented by English pharmacist John Walker in 1826. Known as friction lights, they would burst into flame when struck against a piece of folded sandpaper.

This experiment shows the flammable property of phosphorus using standard household matches. Unlit match heads are clustered together in a Pyrex dish (1). When lit, the red phosphorus-tipped match heads quickly ignite into explosive flame (2).

practical way to light one's oven or cigar, for that matter. However, when flammable phosphorus first started being manufactured on a large scale, it was only a matter of time before someone put two and two together and decided to make phosphorus-tipped matches.

The first self-igniting friction matches were developed in Europe, in the early nineteenth century. They were made out of little sticks of wood, whose heads were covered with a fiery mixture of white phosphorus and other chemicals. When the match head was struck against a surface, the friction provided enough heat to set the match head on fire.

Early matches were called lucifers (another name for the devil). And in fact, their effects were rather sinister. The sparks produced were often very violent, the flames were unsteady, and the odor was unpleasant.

Furthermore, the matches needed to be kept in an airtight box so that they wouldn't self-ignite and explode. Despite these drawbacks—which could include severe burns and accidental poisonings—the new matches were a hit and led to a big rise in the number of smokers.

Red Phosphorus and Matches

Meanwhile, constant breathing in of poisonous phosphorus vapors led to match workers acquiring a disease known as "phossy jaw." The consequences of this terrible condition were that workers' jaws decayed and often had to be removed.

The dangers involved and the harm done to both the people who made matches and those who used them caused scientists to look for a safer alternative to white phosphorus. The search didn't take long. In 1845, an Austrian chemist named Anton von Schrotter discovered red phosphorus, which was much less reactive, and thus much safer than white phosphorus.

Thrilled with this discovery, makers of matches began replacing white phosphorus with red phosphorus in match heads, leading to what has become known as the safety match. They also added a red phosphorus strip on boxes or books of matches that would ignite the match head when struck with the match. This occurs because when you strike a match, the heat caused by the friction converts some of the red phosphorus to white. This tiny amount of white phosphorus then ignites, causing the match head to burn.

Today red phosphorus is still used to make safety matches and matchbook strikers as well as other fiery devices such as flares, caps for cap guns, and, most spectacularly, fireworks. While still dangerous, it is also true that the world would be a much duller place without this original and essential element.

The Periodic Table of Elements

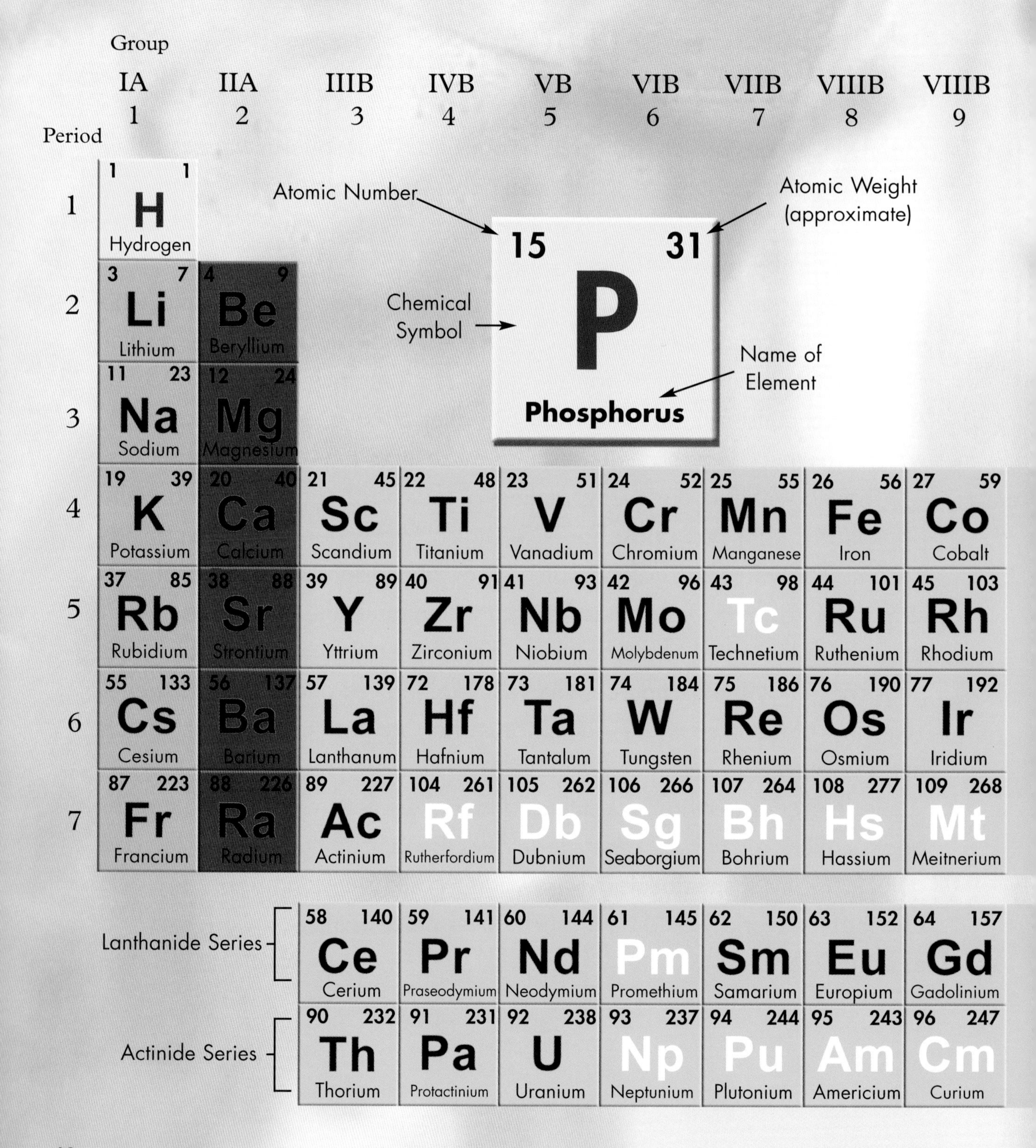

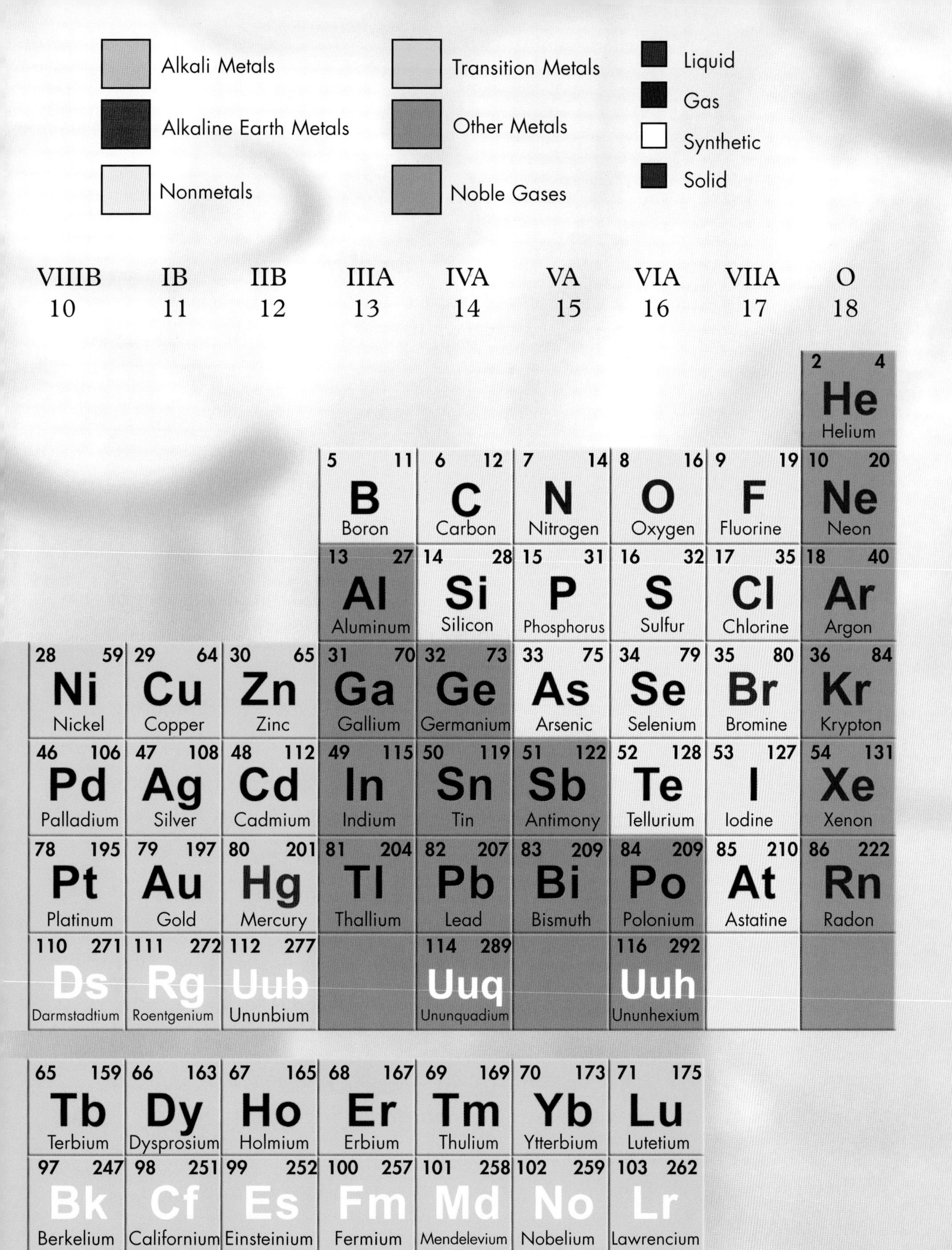
Alkali Metals
Alkaline Earth Metals
Nonmetals
Transition Metals
Other Metals
Noble Gases
Liquid
Gas
Synthetic
Solid
VIIIB 10
IB 11
IIB 12
IIIA 13
IVA 14
VA 15
VIA 16
VIIA 17
O 18
2 4 He Helium
5 11 B Boron
6 12 C Carbon
7 14 N Nitrogen
8 16 O Oxygen
9 19 F Fluorine
10 20 Ne Neon
13 27 Al Aluminum
14 28 Si Silicon
15 31 P Phosphorus
16 32 S Sulfur
17 35 Cl Chlorine
18 40 Ar Argon
28 59 Ni Nickel
29 64 Cu Copper
30 65 Zn Zinc
31 70 Ga Gallium
32 73 Ge Germanium
33 75 As Arsenic
34 79 Se Selenium
35 80 Br Bromine
36 84 Kr Krypton
46 106 Pd Palladium
47 108 Ag Silver
48 112 Cd Cadmium
49 115 In Indium
50 119 Sn Tin
51 122 Sb Antimony
52 128 Te Tellurium
53 127 I Iodine
54 131 Xe Xenon
78 195 Pt Platinum
79 197 Au Gold
80 201 Hg Mercury
81 204 Tl Thallium
82 207 Pb Lead
83 209 Bi Bismuth
84 209 Po Polonium
85 210 At Astatine
86 222 Rn Radon
110 271 Ds Darmstadtium
111 272 Rg Roentgenium
112 277 Uub Ununbium
114 289 Uuq Ununquadium
116 292 Uuh Ununhexium
65 159 Tb Terbium
66 163 Dy Dysprosium
67 165 Ho Holmium
68 167 Er Erbium
69 169 Tm Thulium
70 173 Yb Ytterbium
71 175 Lu Lutetium
97 247 Bk Berkelium
98 251 Cf Californium
99 252 Es Einsteinium
100 257 Fm Fermium
101 258 Md Mendelevium
102 259 No Nobelium
103 262 Lr Lawrencium

Glossary

alchemy The ancient study of different forms of matter with a focus on how to transform basic elements into silver and gold.

atom The smallest particle of an element that retains the properties of that element.

atomic mass The mass or weight of one atom.

atomic number The number of protons in an atom. This number also identifies the element's place on the periodic table.

bond An attraction between two or more atoms or ions that holds them together.

chemistry The study of the properties of matter and how matter changes.

compound A substance made from two or more atoms.

density A substance's mass per unit volume.

ecosystem A system formed by the interaction between a community of living organisms and their physical environment.

electron A negatively charged particle outside the nucleus of an atom.

element A pure substance made from one type of atom.

friction The rubbing of one object or surface against another.

isotopes Atoms of an element that have the same number of protons and electrons but a different number of neutrons.

matter Any substance that has mass (weight) and occupies space.

neutron A tiny particle with no electrical charge found in the nucleus of an atom.

nucleus An atom's center or core, which contains protons and neutrons.

proton A tiny particle with a positive charge located in an atom's nucleus.

refine A process that removes unwanted substances from a pure element.

For More Information

American Chemical Society
1155 Sixteenth Street NW
Washington, DC 20036
(800) 227-5558 or (202) 872-4600
Web site: http://www.acs.org

Center for Science & Engineering Education (CSEE)
Lawrence Berkeley National Laboratory
1 Cyclotron Road, MS: 7R0222
Berkeley, CA 94720
(510) 486-5511
Web site: http://csee.lbl.gov

International Union of Pure and Applied Chemistry (IUPAC)
IUPAC Secretariat
P.O. Box 13757
Research Triangle Park, NC 27709-3757
(919) 485-8700
Web site: http://www.iupac.org

Mineral Information Institute
505 Violet Street
Golden, CO 80401
(303) 277-9190
Web site: http://www.mii.org

Web Sites

Due to the changing nature of Internet links, Rosen Publishing has developed an online list of Web sites related to the subject of this book. This site is updated regularly. Please use this link to access the list:

http://www.rosenlinks.com/uept/phos

For Further Reading

Baldwin, Carol. *Non-metals* (Material Matters). Chicago, IL: Raintree Publishers, 2006.

Beatty, Richard. *Phosphorus* (The Elements). New York, NY: Benchmark Books, 2001.

Blashfield, Jean F. *Phosphorus: Chemical Elements That Make Life Possible*. Chicago, IL: Raintree, 2001.

Newmark, Ann. *Chemistry* (Eyewitness Books). New York, NY: Dorling Kindersley, 2000.

Parker, Steve. *Chemicals & Change* (Science View). New York, NY: Chelsea House Publishers, 2004.

Saunders, Nigel. *Nitrogen and the Elements of Group 15* (The Periodic Table). Chicago, IL: Heinemann Library, 2004.

Stwertka, Albert. *A Guide to the Elements*. 2nd ed. New York, NY: Oxford University Press, 2002.

Zannos, Susan. *Dmitri Mendeleyev and the Periodic Table* (Uncharted, Unexplored, and Unexplained). Hockessin, DE: Mitchell Lane Publishers, 2004.

Bibliography

Brandolini, Anita, Ph.D. *Fizz, Bubble & Flash!: Element Explorations & Atom Adventures for Hands-On Science Fun!* Charlotte, VT: Williamson Publishing, 2003.

Chem4kids. Retrieved January 2007 (http://www.chem4kids.com).

Curry, Roger. "Phosphorus." *Lateral Science*. 2003. Retrieved January 2007 (http://www.lateralscience.co.uk/phos/index.html).

Environmental Literacy Council. "Phosphorus Cycle." Retrieved January 2007 (http://www.enviroliteracy.org/article.php/480.php).

Frank, David V., John G. Little, and Steve Miller. *Chemical Interactions* (Prentice Hall Science Explorer). Upper Saddle River, NJ: Pearson Prentice Hall, 2005.

Mineral Information Institute. "Phosphate Rock." Retrieved January 2007 (http://www.mii.org/Minerals/photophos.html).

Van der Krogt, Peter. "Elementymology & Elements Multidict: Phosphorus." Retrieved January 2007 (http://elements.vanderkrogt.net/elem/p.html).

WebElements. "Phosphorus." Retrieved January 2007 (http://webelements.com/webelements/elements/text/P/key.html).

Index

About the Author

Michael A. Sommers was born in Texas and raised in Canada. After earning a bachelor's degree in English literature at McGill University, in Montreal, Canada, he went on to complete a master's degree in history and civilizations from the Ecole des Hautes Etudes en Sciences Sociales, in Paris, France. For the last fifteen years, he has worked as a writer and photographer.

Photo Credits

Cover, pp. 1, 12, 13, 18, 20, 40–41 by Tahara Anderson; p. 5 © Educational Images/Custom Medical Stock Photo; p. 8 © Derby Museum and Art Gallery, UK/ The Bridgeman Art Library; p. 11 © Science Source/Photo Researchers, Inc; p. 16 © Science Museum/SSPL/The Image Works; p. 24 © Charles D. Winters/Photo Researchers, Inc.; p. 26 Library of Congress Prints and Photographs Division; p. 27 © Tomsich/Photo Researchers, Inc.; p. 28 LifeART image © 2008 Lippincott Williams & Wilkins. All rights reserved; p. 30 © Peter Turnley/Corbis; pp. 32, 38 Mark Golebiowski; p. 34 © Getty Images; p. 36 © Topham/The Image Works; p. 37 © SSPL/The Image Works.

Designer: Tahara Anderson; **Photo Researcher:** Cindy Reiman